Out of Time

Compiled by
Dark Rose Press

Available or Coming Soon
from Dark Rose Press

Destined Drabbles
AT FIRST GLANCE
WORLDS APART
OUT OF TIME

Altered Hearts
LOST SOULS
TOUCH OF SIN
SKIN DEEP

Follow us: linktr.ee/darkrosepress
Website: www.DarkRosePress.com

Jared, Without His Pants

by John Mueter

Few young women in 1832 were familiar with men's small clothes, but Penelope was. She cherished the extraordinary garment she had pinched from the laundry (the name *Hugo Boss* impossibly stitched into the waistband) after the mysterious stranger had visited. There was something so alluring and otherworldly about Jared—she couldn't say exactly what. He was irresistibly attractive and Penelope was hopelessly curious. And desperately needy.

Slipping into his room one evening, uninvited, she discovered him in bed reading, bare-chested, hairy, surprised. His underpants lay on the floor. Penelope was undone by the sight, the thrilling, promising implication of it.

Beyond First Glances

by Betty Pat

The breeze sensually caressed the two shadows sharing the bench in the twilight's penumbra.

"I met you once, right here, and your glance mesmerised me."

"Yes, and I shivered."

"You never answered my call."

"Your heart tells you when you're in danger."

"I had fallen for you immediately, irrevocably."

"But I was married."

"Your face was my last image when old, ill, and I passed away."

"Your image was my last, too. It helped me die peacefully, with hope for my afterlife."

"I'd say, a dream…"

Their insubstantial hands stretched out and touched before their essences vanished in the mist.

Too Late

by Avery Hunter

The clock ticks.

We're strangers, but every night for months I've sat here, your nightly sentry—sunlight's the bane of vampires—watching you sleep. You are so very beautiful...you've stolen my heart.

I know of the cancer that took your mother; it has a hold on you now.

The clock ticks.

Should I take you into my world? Let you go and lose you forever?

The clock ticks.

My lips brush your neck. I feel your ragged pulse and my desire rages.

But, too late, you exhale your final breath. My fangs retract, your soul dissipates.

A tear falls.

The Magic in Her Torch

by Bill Anthony

The machine that brought him sat unguarded in the courtyard. Its strange mechanics glistened in the blood moon.

He had appeared in a blaze of lightning and chaos. As those around her ran in fear, she knew this magic must be hers. To possess it, she would possess him as well. But something went amiss.

Had he worked some charm on her?

Last night, he told her he must return to the distant time from whence he came.

Alone in the courtyard, her torch ignited the kindling beneath his machine. The flames wove their own spell, proclaiming he would stay.

In a Blink

by Brianna Malotke

Your blue topaz eyes held mine, my heart already aching as you once again said goodbye. Your trips grow too infrequent. The potential to ripple time too great.

Our connection deep, our souls woven together. I could spend eternity in your arms, feeling your heartbeat against my naked chest. I'd drown in your ocean-like eyes for just a moment longer together.

Years pass, just a blink for you, but every day an agony for me. I wait for another visit, for more time together. Despite the sorrow in between, I'll never trade anything for the hours we share our love.

Days Long Gone

by Selene Moor

I took refuge from the heat in a roller rink. When my vision cleared, I giggled. The place was suck in the 80s.

I was waiting for an Uber. Might as well enjoy myself.

I was lost in minutes, laughing more as I wheeled around. I didn't notice when a young man joined me until he grabbed my hand and spun me around.

"Ricky?" My high school sweetheart, impossibly young.

He gave me a lopsided grin. "Hey, baby."

I know I tried to leave. I know he pulled me closer. "Stay, where we have all the time in the world."

Wrong Station

by Cara Twomey

She stared at him; a man more handsome than any other she knew. Flustered, she found herself getting off the train at the wrong station and didn't know what to do next.

When the man tipped his hat and asked if she needed assistance, she was dazzled by him. As he stood smiling before her, wondered if she was meant to get off there after all.

She found herself thinking certain thoughts, wicked ones she rarely entertained: *what did he look like underneath those clothes?*

"Yes," she told him, gladly accepting the arm he offered. "I do need you."

Doing Time

by Chris Tattersall

He was given no mercy. No pleas were accepted. He was sentenced to a month behind bars.

Would his love be there for him?

Freedom Day edged closer, until finally it arrived. He woke early, his confinement feeling more restrictive than ever. Release was minutes away.

"I knew you could do it," she said through a proud smile.

He noticed the key around her neck as she knelt.

Through the steel bars restraining his manhood he felt the warmth of her mouth.

"Love you," he whispered.

She backed away, pre-cum dripping from him.

"Prove it. Ask me for another month."

A Long Time Coming

by R.S. Nevil

Craig stared at her.

It had been twenty years. And yet, she still looked the same. Not a hair out of place. Not a wrinkle to her skin.

It was impossible. Yet, there she stood, a smile on her face as she walked towards him.

A rush of emotions hit him in that moment. Emotions he had not felt in twenty years. Emotions he had long since buried. She had come into his life, a whirlwind of fire and ice. Only to disappear without a trace.

She smiled, offering him a knowing look.

"Hello, Craig, it's been a long time."

Summer Solstice

by Cherie Lynae Cabrera Suski

The door handle buzzed under my hand as I entered. The sunrise painted the castle in glowing light. The magic of summer solstice sent me over the threshold of time; from the twenty-first century and into the eighteenth, where my love lived.

"There you are." A freshly bathed, naked man swept me from the ground.

"Alex?" Our room looked the same as it had the night I'd given him my virginity. The dust, and decay gone as he swung me in a circle.

"You found your way back." He covered me with his body and his kisses. "Never leave again."

Differently

by Jenny Logan

"Please, may I go back to my wedding day?" She stepped inside the booth.

"Of course. You'll get about ten hours of it. When would you like to start?"

"Ceremony, please."

"You know you can't change it?"

"Yes. I just want to get to the good bits. Enjoy the guests—few are still alive—and the food. I was too nervous to eat much of it. And the afterwards, of course. Enjoy our first time again."

"Happiest day of your life, was it?"

"It will be. Second time around. No nerves now, you see. No regrets."

"Off you go, then."

The Intimate Details of Time Travel

by Daisy Fortrain

I never know when, where, or how he will appear. He always knows where I'm going to be.

Once he appeared under my desk at work and went down on me while I was on a call. Another time, he was waiting to fuck me in a friend's bathroom during a dinner party. Sometimes he will show up in my bed and just cuddle with me while I sleep.

He told me that he is from the future and has a time machine—but I don't concern myself with the details. I'm having too much fun to worry about that.

For All of Eternity

by Dusty Davis

Addison gasped when she saw the man standing across the street. His wavy brown hair gently blew in the warm breeze. He smiled as he pushed off the street post that he was leaning against, and met her at the curb. He cupped her face and tucked a strand of hair behind her ear.

Shocked, Addison took a step back. He grabbed her by the arm, holding her upright.

"I will wait for you for the rest of time. For all of eternity," the man whispered softly.

Addison gasped as her eyes shot open and light flooded the hospital room.

A Time Shift

by Finnian Burnett

Jana is phasing again. The telltale signs—sudden silences, lapses in conversation. I press against her as tightly as I can, the warmth of her skin telling me this is real, this matters.

Where I come from, women can't be lovers, she says.

I kiss her again, my tongue gliding across her lips. She arches against me, but her heated cries are mixed with grief. Another shift is coming. Whatever slip in time that brought her to me is coming back for her.

She finally shifts with a last kiss and I'm left facing the rest of time without her.

Ghost

by Kailey Alessi

I'm in awe at how beautiful you are. You have aged, yes, but the wrinkles around your eyes and the grey streaks in your hair are stunning.

You lean on a cane as you walk around the house, running a hand over the dusty furniture.

It has been almost seventy years since you were last here.

Since I died.

I wish I could talk to you and tell you how I've never stopped loving you. All these years I've been stuck in this house alone, praying just to see you once more.

I love you, even from beyond the grave..

Time Slip

by Miranda Reynolds

The dense forest swayed in the rising wind. Belle walked a dirt path, savouring the chilled air. It would be Winter soon; too cold for walks in the woods.

The trail broke, and bright sunlight poured across a garden party. A stone mansion towered in the background.

A woman in an old-fashioned dress turned, bloody knife in hand, a dead man at her feet.

Belle's heart lurched with desire. She stepped forward, needing to know this woman. Needing beyond reason to touch her. She stepped forward and the world rippled. Trees replaced stone for miles. As it should be.

Private Lives

by Kyvin Titanite

Hannah's ribs ached. She'd never worn a corset before, but she figured she should try not to raise suspicion with her usual T-shirt and jeans.

Time runs short! Hannah frowned, scanning the bustling Renaissance street for any signs of the noblewoman in blue velvet. She smiled when she saw her nearing the bridge.

I'm the Hannah that she wrote about in her diary. Hannah brushed past a couple and followed the woman that had melted her heart with wistful words of forbidden love.

Finding the diary was no coincidence. It brought me here so I could finally be with her.

Memories

by Gay D. Alson

The first time I saw you, I felt sudden wetness between my legs. When we were introduced, you took my hand and bowed elegantly; but all I could do was visualise what you looked like naked with an erection.

"Why do I have memories of you—of us—when this is the first time we've met?" you murmured.

"I have the same memories," I replied. "At least, I think they're the same."

You smiled. "Some of mine are x-rated."

I smiled. "Mine, too."

"So they aren't real?" you asked.

"Maybe they are," I countered. "We just haven't made them yet."

Bonnie and Claudia

by Kimberly Rei

I started awake at the sound of a nightstick against my cell bars. I kept my eyes closed, schooling my face.

"Time's up!" The guard sounded annoyed.

I sat up, "What?"

"You want outta here or not?"

I scrambled to my feet. Twelve awful, lonely years behind bars, now over. After a flurry of administrative scolding, I stood outside the gates. Free. Breathing fresh air. Still alone. A car horn screeched. I looked over and there she stood, stunningly beautiful.

"Hey, stranger. Wanna ride me?"

I laughed, throwing myself into her arms. "You're here."

"And I still have the haul."

Chase

by Mercy Marie

Time was ticking down. It was going to happen again. Shara could feel it, like something wrapped around her middle, tugging. Pulling her back into another era.

Jax would find her, he always did. As if thinking of him had summoned him. Jax pulled her tight against his body.

Shara gasped, partly from desire, partly from the sensation of being simultaneously pulled in opposite directions.

Leaning down he swept his tongue over the pulse at her throat, tasting her heartbeat.

Slowly, inexorably she began to fade. Time had run out for her here.

"The thrill is in the chase, darling," he quipped with arched brow and crooked grin showing just a hint of fang. "See you soon"

Hard to Get

by Kendal Tomson

Jakob is a prince of his kind, feared and respected. Powerful. He has seen the rise and fall of civilisations, and of stars. Coldly aloof, he stood outside it all, waiting for he knew not what.

Until he caught Andreu's eye. Then predator became prey. Andreu pursued Jakob. Relentless, passionate and charming. For a hundred years, Jakob experienced the full spectrum of human emotions in Andreu's arms.

They were separated by foolish pride and intemperate words. Despairing, Jakob travelled the globe, searching for his lost love. In desperation, he has even travelled through time, seeking, and always coming up empty-handed.

Country Air

by Kara Hawkers

Stepping into the time-travelling machine, I couldn't help but feel a mix of excitement and nerves.

When I materialised in the countryside, I was struck by the untouched beauty of the place. But she eclipsed it all.

"Good day," she greeted me with a smile.

As days turned into weeks, we fell in love. But I knew my time in the past was limited.

"I don't want to leave you," I whispered.

"Then stay." She kissed me passionately, and I knew that I had found my soulmate.

Together, we built a life filled with love, adventure, and the occasional time-travelling escapade.

A Pirate's Plunder

by Hazel Ragaire

Sixteenth century Ireland's western coast's dangerous beauty rivalled the Sea Queen of Connaught's own. Audrey watched her disembark the flagship, tucking the piracy flag away, sun-kissed breasts stretching the leather-bound white blouse.

Gráinne O'Malley tracked Audrey's approach.

"Ye husband allows ye to wear breeches?"

"No husband."

"Just left my second; took the ships though."

Audrey smiled, falling into step with the notorious pirate.

"Seeking another match?"

"Seeking freedom."

Unlacing the leather strings securing her breeches, Audrey looped them around her wrist, offering.

Gráinne's eyes glazed, hands seizing the other wrist.

"I'll plunder *your* treasure," she promised. "Come aboard my ship."

Drawing In

by R.H. Argent

The locket was ancient, the antiquarian claimed. It held a painstakingly painted woman; blood-red lips, auburn hair, eyes that did all the smiling. He asked a ridiculous price, and I paid anyway.

Some would call it a curse, the witch from the locket who comes every night, whose mouth explores every bit of me, devouring all my little deaths, restless and insatiable.

Winter will be here soon, and I don't know how I'll survive. I can barely function. If I'm caught asleep at work again, I'll lose my job.

But I won't give her up.

I've never felt so alive.

Love Letters

by R.S. Nevil

You squeezed my hand three times. Without words, telling me, "I love you." We didn't know when we'd see each other again. My words caught in my throat. With one last embrace, you left.

Over the years, we've exchanged letters, allowing us to fill the pages with expressions of affection, secrets, musings of our days, and even our sorrows. Through paper we shared everything. Oceans lay between us, but our love only deepened.

Maybe one day we'll be face to face again. And when that happens, we'll have the courage to give those sacred words a voice—*I love you.*

The Cost of Discovery

by Bill Anthony

Their experiment was a success. Jacquelyn had travelled in time and returned safely.

Two new printouts lay on his desk. One, the announcement of their engagement. The other, a decades old obituary of a brilliant woman who had developed a scientific process once thought impossible. It was with this process they had built their machine. The photo didn't lie. That woman was Jacquelyn.

The paradox struck a blow that brought tears to his eyes.

Her hand pressed against the window. "Ethan, darling, let me out."

He turned away and flipped the switch to send her back.

Amore Roma

by S.T. May

We died together, holding hands. After that, sex was good but slow, with little urgency. In time, it became more energetic and increasingly imaginative. Gradually as we became younger, our growing passion converted making love into passionate fucking.

Indoors, outdoors, we explored every corner of the world, and each other. Visual sense overwhelmed us. We consumed the full nakedness of each other's bodies until clothing and posture alone satisfied the eye. We downshifted to kissing, every touch smouldered with impassioned yearning.

As college friends we shared classes, until with a handshake we parted forever to discover the innocence of childhood.

A Hundred Orgasms

by Cherie Lynae Cabrera Suski

Everyone tells us how good sex is, but for me, it transcends time.

When I have sex, I experience every encounter at once. Pounding into her, she changes with every jolt. My cock slides into the same woman from a different time with each stroke—my girlfriend, my wife, the mother of my children.

One moment her nails dig into my back as her virginal moans encourage me, the next her sun-kissed hands hold her swollen breasts as I slide to the hilt in her heat. Her cunt squeezes me and I come with the force of a hundred orgasms.

Blood Vow

by Velian Dusk

A thousand years I walked this globe. I watched as trees grew and lands changed. Humans lived and died. Animals went extinct.

I'm still searching for you.

You were by my side at the start. I watched as they caught you, jealous of our immortality. Our freedom. Our love.

I vowed to find you when you were reborn from your ashes. Our hearts are forever entwined, and I can feel warmth once again, though I still shun the sun.

As I followed your scent, my breath caught. I finally found you.

Would you remember me and forsake the sun again?

The Sweetest Fruits

by Jessa Novak

I've eaten pomegranate with Cleopatra and fed figs to Helen of Troy. Marie Antoinette and I once shared delicate pear slices from the gardens of Versailles. Long before the king set his lusty eyes upon Bathsheba, we spent lazy afternoons nibbling raisins and sipping wine. I recall Elizabeth I was partial to fresh peaches, and Grace Kelly would always have an apple to share with me on her movie sets.

I've eaten every kind of melon and berry known to the history of humankind. But by far the sweetest fruit I have ever tasted is the one between your legs.

Law of Attraction

by Jessica O'Brien-Visbisky

The first law of time travel: don't interfere with history. A straightforward, practical regulation.

This criminal investigation assignment appeared no different from those I conducted countless times before. An expedition preceded by an intense examination of character disposition and chronology. I formed an understanding of his every trait.

Quite literally knowing my research assignment better than he knew himself.

I journeyed through history without any hesitation or distrust in my capabilities. I had prepared well.

Research didn't prepare me for his appeal—I was captivated. Enough to alter my inner thoughts and feelings.

Enough incentive to consider breaking the law.

Dying to Love

by Rosetta Yorke

Shrieks pierce the night. My camper van's windows shatter.

I fling open the door. Racing to find the source of the pain-filled screams.

A shadow flits around the tumuli, wringing pale hands. "Death draws near!"

"Ha, ha. Hope you are paying for my windows, joker."

"Death won't be denied." Her grey cloak slips. Silver-haired, she shines like moonlight.

Banshees are real?

Her emerald eyes widen. My heart skips.

"Not you," she keens. *"Take me!"*

Lifeless, she falls.

Where? To what infernal punishment?

I catch her. Kiss her.

Wherever she goes, I go, Death!

Soul-melded, ecstatic, we flit into the night.

Timing is Everything

by Brianna Malotke

Your voice was like honey dripping on my soul. I hung on your every word. Even the most innocent of touches led to intimate affairs between us. The passion consumed us, but every flame fizzles out.

"The timing isn't right."

When the words left your lips, my heart shattered.

I've never loved another like you.

Several years later, in this crowded café, I find myself staring at you over my coffee. My heart pounding as you draw near, yearning for your touch once more. With a smile you say what I've been dreaming about.

"We should have a second chance."

To Unbecome

by Johnathon Heart

He knew her in each siren song of nonexistence. She always came at the end. For her, he would give himself up until nothing of his soul remained. He had mocked those who destroyed themselves for love until he found that he no longer had interest in life without her. If she did not represent life at all, then oh well.

When he found her, he allowed her to suck him dry. She would leave him behind as a husk. When the wind blew, he'd disperse into ash. From the furthest reaches of eternity, he would thank her.

Daily Ritual

by Miranda Reynolds

He saw her every morning hanging clothes on the line out back. He'd been in the house for six months and she hadn't missed a day. Watching her soothed him. Some small part felt guilty, but then she'd look up and smile and his world was perfect.

He tried to ignore that she never spoke. He tried to explain the repetition of her movements—the same clothes hung in the same way.

The sunlight rippled through her, sparkling on the grass that was always green at her feet, no matter the season.

Ghost or not, he was helplessly in love.

Malfunction

by Kailey Alessi

Sometimes I lie awake at night, wondering what went wrong. Was it a calculation? A faulty microchip? A loose rivet?

The possibilities haunt my dreams, jerk me out of a fitful sleep like a fist around my heart. I close my eyes and I see your crooked smile, my skin tingling at the memory of your touch.

I wish I knew where you were, but that knowledge disappeared with you when the time machine blinked out of the present. The scientists say there is nothing to be done, but I won't give up. I will find you. Whenever you are.

Divortium

by Tam Lynn

The tide pulled my shuttle into deeper waters. I'd climbed to the highest point I could, which was not the highest point on the island. No, that was held by...her.

She'd already taken one shot at me and was holding her weapon remarkably steady for someone also holding her abdomen closed.

Her shuttle was parked neatly on a safe patch. She just couldn't get to it alive.

"Let me help you."

"I hate you!"

"Yeah, I got that. But we're going to die here."

She dropped the gun as I lifted her. "Maybe I shouldn't have divorced you."

"Maybe."

Love in Another Time

by Kerri Merriam

I hear tinkling notes from a piano, and I know that it has worked. I am back. I promised I would never leave this house, which allows me to visit.

Following the song, I see the parlour has transformed. A gramophone sits where a computer should be, and there's a piano in the centre of the room that was not there a few moments ago.

My love looks up from his playing, smiling at my entrance. I know his face, and he knows mine. I return his smile. He is from another life, another time. But he is still mine.

Pathways

by Kimberly Rei

The moon shone bright over the standing stones. In the dark hours of the morning, the plains were empty of all living souls, save one.

She waited, staring at one stone as hope bound her heart in a cage. She'd fallen in love here a dozen years before and had spent every moment since researching this perfect night.

The moon began to shift, light moving away. Her soul withered. Had she misjudged?

Behind her, the wind whispered her name. A delicate hand reached. She rushed forward to tangle fingers and step far away.

This time, she was not letting go.

Arles

by Jenny Logan

She drank in the painting and wished herself there—in that lonely bedroom in France. She closed her eyes and imagined lying naked on his bed.

He came home smelling of drink and they made love all night. She told him she loved him, trying to convince him he was worthy of her devotion.

Afterwards, she clung to him. She jerked herself awake again and found she was back in the gallery. The security guard was clearing his throat—it was time for her to leave. Perhaps she would come back here tomorrow, and go there to stay this time.

A Pocket in Time

by Kimberly Wood

The train's whistle startled her awake. Mia wiped the foggy window and noticed a dapper gentleman. He felt familiar to her. When she disembarked, a misty rain settled over the platform, cocooning them. Mia's breath hitched when he approached—she recognised his orchid eyes.

His beard creating friction as he pulled her closer, tentatively brushing her cool lips. Her tongue touched his, a moan escaped her swollen lips. She knew his taste and smell.

"Vaughn," she breathed, her fingers lifting to his jaw.

"My little dove, I've missed you." He clicked the pocket watch closed, sealing himself in her time.

Velvet Dreams

by Kyvin Titanite

Julian swooned, his fists curling around the bedsheets as Denver continued to run their tongue over Julian's shaft. Heat pulsed in Julian's erection, and he yearned for gratification, but he knew the rules. No begging.

Denver's horns glowed, and they looked up through their lashes at Julian. They sensed his desire and delivered a deliberate, seductive glance.

"I won't beg," Julian managed to gasp.

"We'll see about that." Denver smiled devilishly. They traced Julian's nipple with their long tail, then flicked it.

Julian squirmed, feeling the velvet ties brushing his wrists, as another wave of heat pulsed in his erection.

The Superman

by Cherie Lynae Cabrera Suski

I've repeated this day one-hundred-and-sixty times. I've tried everything to escape; explosions, revelations, disruptions. Nothing worked. So I decided I would do something productive. I spent the last sixty days perfecting every position of the Kama Sutra. It never gets old.

Today, we practiced The Superman. I lay on my belly as he entered me, moaning when he braced my arms behind me and lifted. My legs wrapped around his ass, my upper half suspended in midair as my breasts swayed to his rhythm.

If I am going to repeat this day forever, I might as well learn to fly.

Dark Thoughts

by Linda M. Crate

As the days passed, she knew their time together grew shorter. She would meet him again, but she didn't know when or how. So she would enjoy this time as best as she was able.

She didn't want to lose him again.

As they walked out of the beautiful autumn foliage and lie together, she glanced into his orange eyes.

He smiled at her. "I know you're worried, but you need to enjoy the moment."

"Easy for you to say. Aliens live longer than humans," she laughed.

He responded to that by plunging into her, distracting her from dark thoughts.

Wanderlust

by Lori Green

Malpas wraps his silky black wings around my naked body, teasing my nipples with kisses and sharp teeth. Leaving a trail of fire down my skin, his forked tongue plunges deep into the wetness between my legs, my fingers curled tightly in his hair. I come with a shuddering breath, in a cloud of dark feathers.

Hurled down from heaven, he wanders through time, searching for me. Our hunger and need growing with every passing year until we find each other at last. Forever aching in this purgatory of perpetual lust, as once more he is called back to Hell.

Clueless

by Mercy Marie

They came together to hunt a killer. Knowing they played a dangerous game. Clandestine meetings and danger of discovery fuelled the growing tension between them. Stolen glances, heated touches during late nights poring over clues.

"Fuck it." Irene's chair scraped loudly. Straddling Wyatt's lap, her lips found his.

Tension broke in a wave. Clothing disappeared as mouths and hands roamed fiercely. His hands gripped her arse, her legs wrapped his hips. With a groan, he filled her.

She moaned, then whispered, "You got too close, I'm sorry."

Wyatt jerked back in time to see the flash of the knife descending.

Mortal Peril

by Kendal Tomson

From birth Ava was marked to be High Priestess. Insulated—isolated—warned about the dangers of mortals. But Ava was what her mother called wilful. She slipped away after a ritual.

The city was overwhelming, so many people, buildings, noise. Disoriented, she stumbled, barrelling into a cloth-covered wall with shiny buttons. *A mortal!* Panicked, she scrambled back. Looking up, she fell into his eyes. Eyes filled with concern and mirth.

They met frequently. Stolen hours, forbidden kisses, bodies in perfect rhythm.

Ava's initiation approached. Lover or coven. They'd destroy him. Leaving him would destroy her.

Brokenhearted, she chose his safety.

Even in the Un-Life

by M. Leigh

Your hand degloves in my grasp, the cold flesh slippery.
I don't let go.

Just days ago, this hand caressed the sweat on my chest, eagerly clasped my cock.

You struggle to crawl away, murky eyes hungry. A once angelic face, now a sea of oozing sores.

But I only remember your teasing smile. The heady scent of your wild, glistening thighs straddling mine.

Pain sears my insides as the infection from your bite spreads.

This life is over. I hold tighter.

If our fate is to walk the earth as living corpses, I want to walk beside you.

Always.

Desperate Measures

by Kara Hawkers

Marie stared unseeing, willing inspiration to strike. The document blank.

"Bastard," she mumbled.

The man she'd been staring through startled. "Excuse me?"

Marie apologised. They chatted all afternoon, and the next.

One night, the wine and passion flowed. She climbed into his lap, fingers in his hair, her lips on his. He flipped positions. His hips ground against hers, his hand pinning her wrists above her head.

Months passed. Passion became love.

"You're my soulmate." David professed. But he became possessive—jealous rages—a dangerous sickness. Apologetic, loving, passionate after.

Her fear grew to terror. Lacing his wine, she fled.

Break-Out

by Tam Lynn

"He's dying. Maybe a week? Maybe a month," the doctor sounded unconvinced.

The guard stared across the yard at the prisoner watching a pick-up game. He didn't look ill. The guard imagined the grim reaper watching as well. His heart clenched. It wasn't fucking fair.

***

The prisoner startled as his cell door opened. The guard tossed him a uniform. "Get changed. There's no time."

"I can't..."

"Shut up and do it. I didn't kill every man on duty for you to languish."

"Idiot! I'm dying."

"No shit. But you're not dying *here*. I love you too much. Now let's go."

Dear Beloved

by Miranda Reynolds

Closing the diary was like closing off my heart. His words resonated through my soul, leaving a shattered ache. I wanted to open the book again, but it wouldn't help. It never did.

I looked at the paintings on my wall, hoping to lose myself in his eyes. He was so regal, so handsome in uniform. Books and paintings were all I had of him. I would never caress his cheek or lie in his arms.

Long ago, I'd fallen in love with a man dead four hundred years.

I crawled into bed and opened the diary again. "Dear beloved..."

Rekindled Warmth

by Velian Dusk

Once again, Alex was late. He rushed through the rain and onto the busy train platform, hoping to make it through the crowd and into the car before the doors closed.

Sapphire eyes met his from across the platform and rekindled a familiar warmth in his chest.

Markus opened his pocket watch and time stopped. People froze in place, shaking off their umbrellas or stepping forward while clutching their hats. The raindrops had even paused in their descent from the sky, holding the form of crystallised meteors in the air between the two men.

Alex smiled and ran toward Markus.

Love and War

by Rosetta Yorke

Another arrow pierces my side. My shield grows heavy.

Before me, hordes of perfidious oath-breakers; behind me, my king stands alone.

I fight on.

Lightning bolts split the sky, silhouetting the corpse-strewn battlefield and my blood-blackened sword. Mighty hooves thunder from on high.

Randalin!

Helmeted, with copper hair streaming behind her, my Valkyrie tosses me a horn of mead. Stormracer snorts, plunging and rearing, slashing, and biting, trampling the damned till none remain.

We salute my king.

Randalin laughs, exultant. "It's time, my love." She swings me up behind her.

I clasp her burnished breastplate.

Together, we ride.

To Valhalla!

Blast from the Past

by Jenny Logan

Paul arrived too late to raise the alarm.

He pulled the woman closest into a doorway. The blast blew him off his feet. Again. He held her, helped calm her down.

"My name's Susie." She shook his hand. "You saved my life."

"Paul. It's one worth saving, I trust?"

Susie lived alone, asked Paul to stay with her for the night. He held her close, singing into her hair.

Provided he didn't bump into his younger self in this timeline, there was no reason not to stay, was there?

He'd lived through this war once; he could do it again.

Café Crossroads

by Selene Moor

As liminal spaces go, the coffee shop stood unique. People came and went quickly. Those who lingered soon felt a press to move along, tend chores, call an old friend.

A woman sat in a corner, sipping and watching the door. One hand rested under her thigh, fingers curled around an iron blade.

The smell of cotton candy rose. No one noticed the beautiful creature appearing next to her.

"It's too late for that, love. Let go."

Musical notes. Impossible to ignore. Impossible to run from. It was exhausting to try.

The blade clattered to the floor as they vanished.

By the Comet's Glow

by Kimberly Rei

The comet had been crossing the night sky for weeks, slow and bright. The light was fading. This was their last chance.

Two brides stood between two trees, hand in hand under the soft glow, faces alight with love. Above them, a man hung by ropes, whimpering. His arms and legs strained against the bindings.

A priestess crouched on a wide limb beside the man, chanting the wedding vows. With the last word, she drew a knife across his throat, silencing the whines and blessing the brides in the rain of his blood.

They would live long and happy. Together.

Letters

by Kailey Alessi

I'm in the archives, flipping through a stack of historic letters. My heart is beating out of my chest. Finally, at the bottom of the stack, is a letter addressed to me.

I set aside the other letters with a shaking hand. Your words wash over me like a wave. You say you love me, that you miss me. That you aren't angry. Tears fill my eyes and fall onto the fragile paper, blurring the ink.

I wipe my eyes and prepare to return to the broken time machine, the seemingly never-ending repairs, a silent prayer on my lips.

Soon.

Hatfields and McCoys

by Selene Moor

Gunfire sounded over the hills. Jonce clutched Roseanna closer, staring into her eyes. Their families were caught in an eternal war, trapped for all time in hatred and misunderstanding. The moon hung fat and bright overhead.

Jonce trailed fingers through Roseanna's hair. "My love. I will gaze upon you for all time."

She kissed his hand, shaking her head, "For all time. For no time. Until the moon falls from the sky or wanes above."

They knew the curse too well, every moment carved into their spectral hearts.

As night bitterly gave way to day, gunfire faded over the hills.

Finally

by Shawna Renée Lewis

I float through the fog watching you. My heart stops as you turn and look my way. You're trying to see me, but you can't yet. I breathe a heavy sigh of sadness. I know you can sense me.

As we near the place you visit daily, I stop. You continue your walk to my grave. You lie on the dirt with tears falling. You look up in surprise. Finally able to see me.

"But, you're dead," he says.

"So are you. Took you long enough to recognise that," I said.

He smiles at me. We have eternity now.

Your Smile

by S. Jade Path

Your first kiss roared through me like fire, obliterating every kiss that had come before. You looked

into my eyes and saw all of me. You moved inside me and I felt you even deeper in my soul then you were in my body.

"I love you." Your whisper in my ear sent shivers cascading through me.

You promised forever. You vowed a future filled with love, adventure, and passionate nights.

When you left, you took part of me with you. But, I kept part of you.

Memories of your crooked smile can still lift the corners of my lips.

Come Find Me

by Velian Dusk

Lucas held Eason close, admiring how their bodies fit together so perfectly. He caressed Eason's cheek with his fingertips, tracing the length of his face from temple to jaw. He frowned when he noticed the drag of his hand, the way the action slowed down as he traced his lover's jaw.

"There's never enough time," he sighed, saddened that their intimate moment was once more interrupted as time reset.

"There's always next time," Eason replied with a playful smile.

"I'm always afraid I won't find you," Lucas confessed, kissing Eason's hand.

"But you did." Eason reassured him. "And you will."

Even Ice Melts

by Nicole Kay

She left whispers and turning heads in her wake, but Mia never let her annoyance show. She couldn't afford to. Mafia princesses had to be untouchable.

But tonight she wanted to be touched. She'd heard he was back. That's why she was at this gathering of mafiosos.

Mia's icy gaze swept the room, cataloguing, dismissing—hoping he'd be here.

It had been years, maybe he'd forgotten her. She spotted him across the room.

Dominic. Time stood still. Her heart raced, melted.

His eyes met hers, his sardonic mask slipping for a heartbeat, desire flared in his eyes.

He hadn't forgotten.

Window

by Jenny Logan

Lizzie sang, making stripes in the carpet with the vacuum. She jumped as she locked eyes with the window cleaner, swaying slightly in his harness. Removing her headphones, they held each other's gaze as he lowered himself to her level and put his hand on the pane leaving a print. She pressed her palm against his, imagining warmth transferring. She felt they were the only two people in the world. Tears fell from their eyes.

Climbing onto the ledge, all she wanted was to pull him inside. If only they had met before the fall that had taken his life.

At Long Last

by Paula MacDonald

"I want her now," Ren demanded.

"What will you give me?" The Chairman, an Eternal, controlled every Earthly relationship.

"All the rest of my lives."

"Granted." Sucker. Love was an illusion.

"Thank you." Worth it. His desire for her, his soul mate, had grown to unquenchable levels. He found, then lost, her in every life. His heart contracted, as he recalled returning from France, safe after the war. Only to discover she and the children had perished in a bombing the week before.

The Chairman raised his hands.

Ren materialised in a bookstore entrance, as she was exiting. He smiled.

New Beginning

by Brianna Malotke

We were young and in love. We wore our rose-coloured glasses and pretended everything was fine. Eventually, we knew we had to break up, grow up, and try to move on.

Summers came and went. I never found anyone who I loved so deeply. Your emerald eyes haunted my dreams. I became my own person, had my own accomplishments, and moved time zones. The only thing I ever felt was missing was you.

Of all places, we find ourselves staring at the same painting. And in that museum, we decide to try again. A new beginning for us, together again.

Technological Wonder

by Tam Lynn

I stared at the face of my beloved, so still. No tears fell. I had no room for them. And no reason. My hands, bloody to the wrists, pulled a pristine white sheet over her face.

"Think they bought it?"

I turned to stare at the face of my beloved, very much alive, "Maybe. Let's not chance it. The car's around back."

Our cross-country rampage had come to an abrupt end the only way it could—with Guinevere dead and me mysteriously vanished. We turned our back on the clone and ran for our lives.

Technology was a wonderful thing.

Time Framed

by R.H. Argent

We made love at the best vantage points, grandest hotels, fucking as Rome burned, cumming as the guillotine dropped... Until the moment I arrived, and you didn't.

We had a plan, an anchor point, but hadn't thought it through. Time's a slippery bitch and we shouldn't have fucked with her so often. It's like being in an old film, always one frame apart.

I've seen the odd note. "Where are you?" Accusatory, 'til the realisation sank in. "I'm sorry. I love you."

I won't give up. I'll keep returning, in the hopes that one day our timelines will again intertwine.

Disastrous Devotion

by Jessa Novak

We held each other as we choked on ash in Pompeii. I kissed your brow as you succumbed to plague, knowing I would follow. You squeezed my hand as the lights flickered on the Titanic, water running under the door.

I see you at the supermarket. What if this time I let you go? Went this whole life without your lips on mine, bodies locked together, hearts thundering? To spare us a terrible end, doomed from the moment we meet?

I catch up to you, tap your shoulder. You turn with an unguarded smile.

I'm sorry, I'm not strong enough.

Golden Age

by Jenny Logan

The doorbell rang. I opened it to find a sixty-year-old version of the young man who'd left only two days ago. My heart raced and my hands trembled.

"My goodness, you've not changed a bit." He chuckled nervously.

I flung my arms around him. "How did it go?"

"The mission was successful. The earth will keep turning a little while longer, but I am changed, as you can see."

"I don't care. You're my husband and I love you no matter what." His eyes were the same, his hair greyer.

"What about—"

"The kids will get used to it."

Reunion

by Miranda Reynolds

The face staring back from the slick magazine was unfamiliar, but I still knew him. My soul knew him, knew those eyes. Lifetime over lifetime, he was always there. I'd learned quietly to look for him. He never remembered. Our love. Our lovemaking. For him, it was always the first time.

I liked it that way. It added spice to what could be eons of boredom.

I tucked my tools into a designer bag: cuffs, rope, knife. Gag.

It had become my private game, finding new ways to remind him. His confusion and fear would be the best spice yet.

Take Me

by Selene Moor

Moonlight shone at the crossroads and nowhere else. A young man waited, clutching a guitar. As clouds danced overhead, his age shifted. Older. Younger. So much older. He swayed, but held his ground.

He had agreed, after all.

The air sparked with the sharp scent of a cigar. A deep, ragged voice brushed his ear as a skeletal hand ran over his chest and down to grip aching flesh. He whimpered.

"Are you ready?"

A nod. He'd been ready thirty years ago when he struck the deal, but he lacked courage then. His fingers closed over bones, squeezing.

"Take me."

Out of the Zone

by Velian Dusk

Felix covered himself with a blanket and rose, standing in the yellow sunlight that filtered in through the window.

"Must you leave so soon?" Jesse frowned, watching his lover on his laptop screen. "I just returned."

"The morning comes quick," Felix chuckled and glanced at the webcam.

"For you." Jesse yawned quietly.

"Right. The sun just set for you."

"Well, if you 'd rather come back in time, you could catch a flight back home," Jesse teased.

"These time zones make the distance between us greater." Felix sighed. "Why don't you be the time traveller and join me in the future?"

Goodbye My Love

by R.S. Nevil

Margret stared at him.

Her breathing coming in sharp, rapid gasps.

It was almost time. Her life was nearing its end.

"I don't understand," she said. "You never changed."

Alfred gave her a sad, knowing smile.

"It's a long story," he said.

They were supposed to grow old together, to love and live out their lives.

That was not what had happened. He was not destined to die. Not now. And not for a long time to come. Still, he would feel her death as deeply as he felt the others.

She would be with him forever.

"Goodbye, my love."

Catching On

by Kimberly Rei

The bartender watched silently as the woman at the end of the counter fended off relentless attempts for her affections.

She looked like she tumbled out of a noir film, lush and clad in red silk. The 'tender refilled her drink silently and stepped into the back to catch her breath. It wasn't appropriate to lust after the customers. Worse to actively hit on them. She needed a moment to reclaim professionalism.

The door clicked shut. Noir snuggled against the bartender, curves pressed close.

"I've been here every night for months. I'm tired of waiting for you to catch on."

Love is the Ultimate Sacrifice

by Renee Cronley

Magic separates me from Poppy. Her father cast her into a realm below the sea to keep us apart. He used the sand where she last stood and put it in an hourglass. I only see her for an hour each day as a reflection in the water, along with the daughter I never got to hold.

Their image slowly fades as the sand disappears.

The sand slips away and my heart shatters. Spilling from my eyes, sending ripples where their image swam.

I reach in to pull them out.

I fall in, drowning. We spend my last moments together.

Love Burns

by Rosetta Yorke

Flames lick my shoes.

Look at me, Lord Marr, so aloof on your dais. Were I truly a witch, I would curse you to burn too, for all eternity.

The world rumbles. Shakes. Onlookers flee, screaming.

An ebony, two-wheeled charger leaps out of the sky. Its black-leather knight slashes my bonds with a hunting knife. He shoves up his visor.

Lord Marr?

No. Younger. Eyes wiser. Mouth kinder.

"Climb aboard, Angel. Seven lifetimes and three fortunes have gone into Harley's flying circuits."

His blazing love ignites my own.

Skirts hiked, I clasp his waist.

We roar up into the heavens.

Midnight Call

by Jessa Novak

At midnight I pick up the phone and turn the rotary. It rings twice.

"Hey, sweetheart." That voice alone melts me.

"Are you looking at the stars?"

"Yep. I drove out to a field to see them bright and clear." I shake my head. I'm told someday telephones won't need wires, but it seems impossible.

"I'm lying next to you, squeezing your hand."

"I'm tucking your hair behind your ear. I'm kissing your cheek."

"I'm telling you, 'I love you.'" I wait. It's the first time I've said it.

"I love you, too." The words reach me across the years.

Tangled in Time

by Miranda Reynolds

An arch of vines and twisting leaves stood deep in the forest, waiting patiently. In time, wandering lovers stumbled upon it, their delighted exclamations scaring the birds from the trees.

As a full moon rose, before the sun set, one stepped through. When he tried to step back, he found his way blocked.

He pounded his fists bloody. His lover beat on the portal, tearing at it. A thorn pricked finger. His lover fell into an endless sleep.

Decades later, the eternally young man sobbed, staring at the skeleton curled at the base of the arch. Both trapped in time.

Playing Tourist

by Tam Lynn

The kiss was camouflage. We'd both tried to steal the same gem; now we were both trying not to get caught. Robbing a museum in daylight was dangerous. I loved the risk. Apparently, he did, too.

We pressed against a wall. My hand tangled in his hair, his arm around my waist. Alarms screamed all around us.

"Oy! You can't do that here! It's a bloody crime scene. Out! Now!"

I blushed; he apologised. Just tourists making out. Perfectly harmless.

We fled, hands clasped, ruby caught between us.

Around the corner, he pulled me close and kissed me again. "More."

Unlawful

by Kara Hawkers

Felipe sat at the bar, full of whisky, trying to think of a way to protect his MC.

A sultry, laughter-filled voice pulled him from dark thoughts. "Whisky won't solve your problems."

"No, but science says it's a solution. So..." He tipped his glass.

Felipe's control was as notorious as his MC, but that night started a reckless romance that enraged the restless gang. Already under surveillance and he picks the governor's niece...

Everyone tried, but their love was undeniable. Their passion unquenchable.

Felipe was gunned down during a raid—shooter unknown.

With new leadership, the state's case mysteriously dissolved.

Ascent of Man

by S.T. May

When I left, we were in our twenties. I remember how we spent the night before my departing launch strapped into all the necessary tubes and tension bands, tethered together, floating in the conjugal bunk that enabled orbital sex. We laughed when you triggered your heartbeat alarm every time you came inside me.

When I boarded the near-lightspeed mission, the scent of you lingered in my flight suit. That reminder of our final coupling kept me warm across the cold emptiness of deep space. I returned one year older, and fifty years after your death.

Time dilation is a bitch.

Forever

by S. Jade Path

The straps around your wrists pull and you buck against me. I nearly tumble from my seat on your thighs. My fingers wrap tighter around the throbbing core of you. Your moans thrill me, the desperate pleading an aphrodisiac. I shiver in delightful anticipation. The sticky warmth of your essence drips down the backs of my hands. You pulse in my hand as I tug.

You promised me forever. But my devotion wasn't enough. *I* wasn't enough. First you stole my heart—it beat only for you. Then you walked away, tearing it from my chest.

Now it's my turn.

Every Ten Years

by Shawna Renée Lewis

Every ten years you walk through that portal, never aging as fast as me. You say you love me, but I am forbidden to go to your realm. Wasted love is what I call it. I can't love anyone but you. So, I wait for you every ten years.

I know that this is our last visit. I have aged too much. I won't be around for the next meeting. He just smiles and holds his right hand out. As our palms touch the electricity is overwhelming. I glance at the mirror in the hallway. I am young again.

Painted Memories

by Miranda Reynolds

I sat in the museum, heart aching as I stared at the painting. She was beautiful. Long blond curls caught in the wind, even longer white dress stark against the riot of wildflowers. I'd been here before, so many times.

I felt as if I knew her, as if I had lost her. Tears burned my eyes.

She turned to me, the paint twisting with her. A hand reached out.

"Come back to me, Anna."

Naught but a whisper against my ear. My name. Her lips. I shivered, remembering her touch. But, how?

The date on the painting read 1654.

The Clock Decides

by Tess P.

With trembling fingers, she traces pensive eyebrows, hollow cheeks, the outline of that determined jaw. She continues one soft stroke down his warm neck, resting on her favourite spot. He has always joked about her healing hands, especially when his muscles ached after football with the guys. She circles them now over his abdomen, closing her eyes, willing her goodness to somehow break through his illness. She flops her head onto his bare chest, beaten, raven curls blanketing his body, just how he likes.

The clock ticks. Two breaths…pause…she kisses his lips as he sighs his final farewell.

By Any Means

by Kimberly Rei

"I find you fascinating."

I wanted to slap the smirk right off that too-pretty mouth. The gun in his hand changed nothing. The portal behind him was a different story. I watched it slowly close, time ticking away as he played cute.

Damn it, he was cute.

If I was going to get by, I'd have to surprise him.

I threw my arms around him, planting my lips on his and trying to turn us both. I didn't expect him to wrap around me. I certainly didn't expect to enjoy the kiss.

We both tumbled through as the portal closed.

The Reunion

by Cherie Lynae Cabrera Suski

He slid into bed beside his wife, taking in her youth. She looked so healthy, so beautiful. He ran his thumb over her lips and she sighed, her eyes blinking open.

"I thought you were out of town." Her voice brought his heart to his throat.

His current self was indeed out of town.

"I missed you." He held back tears. She would die of cancer in six years. He had forgotten what her face looked like. He crushed her to his chest, his mouth crashing down on hers with desperation. "Tell me that you love me."

"I love you."

Whisper My Name in Bedsheets

by Tiffiny Rose Allen

Your hand trailing along my arm, whispered kisses as I lie in bed, smiling to my heart's content with sleep still lingering. I open my eyes slowly, and you vanish.

I hear you whispering my name through time; a week...a month...a year past. A barrier of agonies keeps us apart

I place my hand where I had felt yours, a wave of memories bringing me back. Bittersweet remembrances of rolling in sheets and smothering each other in affection. Hands gripping my thighs as I come up for air and try to breathe through you...to inhale you fervently.

Fairy Tale Lover

by Selene Moor

It was the tenth day of waters rising. The island wasn't "just flooded" as the government kept trying to tell us. It was sinking, and we were stranded. No one was coming to rescue us.

I thought of my parents and cousins. Of my first love. I remembered her arms around me, keeping me safe.

Water lapped at the edge of the porch. I sat on my roof. I could climb higher into the hills, but why? I'd rather stay with my home.

Beating wings pounded above me. She smiled as she landed. "Miss me? Let's get out of here."

If Only

by R.S. Nevil

Do you believe in love at first sight?

I do.

But it wasn't until Geraldo that I knew it was true.

If only he knew how I felt about him. Then he could love me. And we could be together.

Even now, as he walks towards me, I can feel the butterflies inside of me.

Will it always be this way? Will he always make me feel like this? How long will these feelings last?

He is the man of my dreams. So handsome and charming. He is the boy every girl wants. And one day he'll be all mine.

Sweeter than Success

by Rosetta Yorke

Seize the Time-Orb. Run to my dirigible. Clamber in, skirts flapping and corset heaving. Spin the dials. Propellers whirring, she rises.

Success tastes sweet.

The sky darkens. *Not the Imperium, in pursuit already? Relax. Only an air-scavenger.*

My pistol fires. The harpy shrieks, flumps onto my gas-balloon, tumbles down like eddying smoke, thuds onto the deck. Flip her over with my boot.

Obsidian eyes glint up at me, wickedly alive—luring…longing…lusting…

Mutual passion rocks my ship.

We could activate the Time-Orb, travel *back*, destroy the Imperium's inception. Instead, we travel *forwards,* choosing infinite togetherness, beyond time itself.

Love tastes sweeter!

Perfect Recall

by S.T. May

Crossing the time portal, I fall, whipped by tree branches.

I awake on furs in a smoky cave, naked, my head cradled in a Neanderthal woman's lap. She caresses my jaw and brings her lips to taste mine. Her fingers stroke my nipples before moving downwards, mutual attraction bypassing language.

Decades later, her profile bulging with our seventh child; we climb our newly completed temple pyramid to the location where my fourth-floor laboratory had once been. The portal reappears, as it does every year, sucking us forward through time into the crystal ant's nest that our hybrid descendants call 'City'.

Closure

by Tam Lynn

Botanicals are wonderful in their simplicity. They don't lie. They don't taunt, or betray, or leave one at the altar. They are direct, giving every warning a person needs.

The thing about plants, the very best thing, is the variety. Something for everyone. They can heal or they can harm. Sometimes, the same plant can do both. Isn't that fascinating?

I know it's been years, but I said I'd come for you. I just didn't say when. I'm grateful you chose to meet with me, after everything. Closure is good for the soul, don't you think?

How's the tea, dear?

Survival for Love

by R.S. Nevil

George stared at the photo.

The blonde-haired woman staring back at him, smiling. It made his heart clench. She was the love of his life, the only woman he had ever truly loved.

And now, he was gone, banished to this forsaken place, sent back to this forsaken time.

He tucked the photo back into his pocket, shoving it away for later. If he ever wanted to see Eve again, he would first have to survive.

He picked up his rifle, knowing what that entailed, knowing what he had to do.

For the battle of Charleston was about to begin.

As the World Spins

by Velian Dusk

The beginning of the "Wedding March" interrupted our conversation.

"This was not the time, Carson," Ryan huffed. "You should have told me how you felt before. We can't go back in time—"

"We don't have to go back," Carson reached out and took Ryan's hand. He swallowed, his heart in his throat, as he made one last plea to his lover. "But you don't have to go forward either."

Ryan glanced at the door that would lead him down the aisle, away from the man he truly loved. "But we can't just stay here."

"We can create our own timeline."

Gone

by Kerri Merriam

I sat on the bus, silently cursing my car trouble. Then I saw her. She gazed out the window. I swore I knew her, knew I needed to speak to her, and would regret it forever if I did not.

My courage had almost been worked up when the bus stopped, and she stood to leave. I watched her go—frozen. Abruptly I sprang up, running to catch her like I had run to catch the bus.

This seemed far more urgent.

"Wait!" I called, but when I jumped from the bus and scanned the crowd—she was already gone.

Authors

Avery Hunter

Author of *Too Late*

Avery Hunter invented writing, the quokka (but not its propensity for sacrificing its young to predators), and mudguards for bicycles (after an unfortunate incident one muddy Monday morning). Now they teach tarantulas how to make a perfect mimosa.

Website: linktr.ee/AuthorAveryHunter

Betty Pat
Author of *Beyond First Glances*

Bill Anthony

Author of *The Magic in Her Torch* and *The Cost of Discovery*

Bill Anthony is the pen name used by Bill Bibo Jr when writing in the Romance genres and featured in *Lucky Stars (Bones Hollow Book 6)* published by Paramour Ink. Follow "Bibo Madness" at billbibojr.com. It's always a work in progress. And it's always fun.

Website: billbibojr.com

Brianna Malotke

Author of *In a Blink, New Beginning* and *Timing is Everything*

Brianna Malotke is a member of the Horror Writers Association. You can find her most recent work within *Sirens Call Publications, Under Her Skin, The Dire Circle, Balm 2* and *Cherish*. Her debut poetry collection, *Don't Cry on Cashmere*, debuted Fall 2022 with Ravens Quoth Press.

Website: malotkewrites.com

Cara Twomey

Author of *Wrong Station*

Cara Twomey has an AA in Liberal Arts & Sciences. Her short fiction is, or will soon be, published in anthologies from Dark Rose Press, Belanger Books, Dark Rose Press, Iron Faerie Publishing, Shacklebound Books, and Black Ink Fiction. She lives in New York.

Instagram: @c.v.twomey

Cherie Lynae Cabrera Suski

Author of *The Superman, Summer Solstice, A Hundred Orgasms,* and *The Reunion*

A labour and delivery nurse, Cherie is following her dream of becoming an author. She recently published her short story, "The Betrothal Trials", with Dragon Soul Press, and her poem, "Why We Love", with Fifth Wheel Press. She is now querying her debut novel, *I Am Armageddon.*

Website: DarlingLynae.com

Chris Tattersall

Author of *Doing Time*

Chris is a Health Service Research Manager from Wales, UK. He lives with his wife Hayley and Border Collie Toby in Pembrokeshire. He enjoys fishing, kayaking and cycling around the west coast of Wales and is a self-confessed flash fiction addict with some publication and competition success.

Website: fusilliwriting.com

Daisy Fortrain

Author of *The Intimate Details of Time Travel*

Daisy Fortrain lives on a ski resort in British Columbia, Canada, and enjoys writing, traveling and the outdoors.

Dusty Davis

Author of *For All of Eternity*

Dusty Davis was born and raised in the small city of East Liverpool, Ohio. He lives there with his wife, two children, and his evil cat, Zazzles. Dusty is an author of poetry and horror fiction. He currently has two short story collections available. Readers can interact with Dusty on all the social media platforms.

Finnian Burnett

Author of *A Time Shift*

Finnian Burnett is a college instructor and flash fiction writer. They live in British Columbia with their wife and Lord Gordo, the cat.

Website: finnburnett.com

Gay D. Alson

Author of *Memories*

In addition to being a technical writer (now retired), She also sold stories for several years to a now-defunct women's market. These days she's writing sci-fi, fantasy, and mystery.

Hazel Ragaire

Author of *A Pirate's Plunder*

Only ideas outnumber the books in Hazel's home. Breathing life into monster monstrosities, dark desires, and the just plain weird with a dash of horror or a sprinkle of sci-fi is kinda what she does. See what her brain dreams up at www.hazelragaire.com.

Twitter: @HRagaire

J
enny Logan

Author of *Window, Blast from the Past, Differently, Arles,* and *Golden Age*

Jenny Logan is based in Edinburgh. You can find her on *Friday Flash Fiction, 50-Word Stories* and *Carrot Ranch* websites. She has work selected by Iron Faerie Publishing.

Facebook: @JennyLogan

Jessa Novak

Author of *The Sweetest Fruits, Midnight Call,* and *Disastrous Devotion*

Jessa Novak (she/they) is a queer writer of romance, fantasy, and paranormal fiction by day, and a labour and delivery nurse by night. A Colorado-to-Washington transplant, you can also find her hiking, camping, snuggling her cat, and unable to read or listen to just one book at a time.

Website: www.darlinglynae.com/jessa-novak

Jessica O'Brien-Visbisky

Author of *Law of Attraction*

Jessica O'Brien-Visbisky is an eighteen-year-old university student and writer residing in British Columbia. She has participated in multiple spoken-word poetry and writing competitions within her school district. When not writing she also enjoys dancing, musical theatre, and public speaking.

John Mueter

Author of *Jared, Without His Pants*

John Mueter is a pianist, composer, educator, translator, and writer residing in Kansas City, Missouri. His short fiction has appeared in many journals, most recently in *The First Line,* The Corona Book of Ghost Stories and *The Mason Street Journal*, poetry in The Train River Anthology and *The Bombay Literary Magazine.*

Website: johnmueter.wordpress.com

Johnathon Heart

Author of *To Unbecome*

Johnathon Heart is the pseudonym of a prolific editor. Their horror pieces have been featured in *Bleed Error* and are upcoming on the Thirteen Podcast, and in Aurelia Leo's FABLE Anthology. Their fantasy/romance pieces have been published by Factor Four and are upcoming from Grendel Press,

Kailey Alessi

Author of *Ghost, Malfunction,* and *Letters*

Kailey Alessi has lived in Michigan, Kentucky, and most recently, Idaho. An anthropology graduate student by day, by night she writes dark fiction. Her short fiction has been published in several anthologies.

Website: kaileyalessi.com

Kara Hawkers

Author of *Country Air, Unlawful* and *Desperate Measures*

Kara Hawkers is a poet and author of short, dark fiction. As Editor-in-Chief, Kara devotes most of her time to operating The Ravens Quoth Press, along with her partner. If left unsupervised, you'll find her dabbling in other arts. Just 3 ravens in a trench coat.

Website: linktr.ee/TheRavensQuothPress

Kendal Tomson
Author of *Hard to Get* and *Mortal Peril*

Kerri Merriam

Author of *Gone*

Kerri Merriam is a Canadian author of many genres and has been writing stories and poems since childhood. She has self-published two books and is working on her second novel.

Website: kerrimbuckton.com

Kimberly Rei

Author of *Bonnie and Claudia, By Any Means, Pathways, By the Comet's Glow,* and *Catching On*

Kimberly Rei does her best work in the places that can't exist...the in-between places where imagination defies reality. With a penchant for dark corners and hooks that leave readers looking over their shoulder, she is always on the lookout for new ideas and new ways to make words dance.

Website: reitales.com

Kimberly Wood

Author of *A Pocket in Time*

Kimberly Wood wears many hats from beta reading for published writers to help lead an active writing group. She enjoys reading and writing paranormal and fantasy romances. Besides her love of sweets, she loves being creative. Kimberly lives in the Midwest with family and their sweet dog.

Kyvin Titanite

Author of *Private Lives* and *Velvet Dreams*

Kyvin Titanite is a genderqueer, transgender writer who specialises in dark fantasy fiction and poetry. He recently self-published *Love in Flight*, their debut poetry book in February 2022. They have co-authored two fantasy books in the Crimson Plumes Series, the first of which was published on Amazon in August 2020.

Website: vincenthunterofficial.wordpress.com/about/side-projects/kyvin-titanite/

Linda M. Crate

Author of *Dark Thoughts*

Linda M. Crate's works have been published in numerous magazines and anthologies both online and in print. She is the author of eleven published chapbooks, four full-lengths, and three micro-chaps. She has a novella, also, called *Mates* (Alien Buddha Publishing, March 2022).

Instagram: @authorlindamcrate

Lori Green

Author of *Wanderlust*

Lori Green is a Canadian writer who has been writing dark tales since she first picked up a pen. She studied English Literature at the University of Western Ontario, and her work has been published at Black Hare Press and Poetry Undressed. She is currently working on her first novel.

M. Leigh

Author of *Even in the Unlife*

M. Leigh is a women's fiction horror writer from Woodinville, Washington. Her stories have been published with Flame Tree Press and Black Hare Press. She is currently working on her first novel.

Mercy Marie

Author of *Chase* and *Clueless*

Miranda Reynolds

Author of *Painted Memories, Reunion, Time Slip, Daily Ritual, Dear Beloved,* and *Tangled in Time*

Miranda Reynolds loves chai lattes, storms, and fuzzy blankets. When she's not arguing with Life, she's lining up words and whipping them into twisted tales. In Miranda's dream-filled opinion, the world needs more wonder, more shivers, and more sensual adventures.

Website: mirandareynolds.com

Nicole Kay

Author of Even Ice Melts

Mx Nicole Kay is a multi-genre author of dark fiction. A caffeine and snark-fuelled Chaotic Switch, who is fond of cuddles and horror films with her partner. Otherwise, Nicole can be found diligently granting wishes and breaking hearts in her role as Editor-in-Chief at DARK ROSE PRESS.

Facebook & Twitter: @mxdrkprincess

Paula MacDonald

Author of At Long Last

Paula MacDonald has held many jobs over the years—financial analyst (not recommended), public library worker (so great), and mom (most rewarding). A cancer diagnosis caused her to rethink her life's path and now she is actively pursuing her passion of writing.

R.H. Argent

Author of Time Framed and Drawing In

R.H. Argent lives in Nottingham, UK, and co-founded the Sutton Bonington Campus Creative Writing Group as a staff wellbeing event. R.H. has had several works of flash fiction published, including in Dark Rose Press' *At First Glance,* and *Worlds Apart* anthologies, and in the *81 words,* and QSF's *Ink,* anthologies.

R.S. Nevil

Author of Survival for Love, Goodbye My Love, A Long time Coming, Love Letters and If Only

R.S. Nevil is an avid reader and author. He mainly writes science fiction, while also dabbling in other genres. R.S. spends most of his free time reading, writing, and trying to perfect his craft, coming up with new and fantastic tales of werewolves, vampires, and anything else supernatural.

Renee Cronley

Author of Love is the Ultimate Sacrifice

Renee Cronley is a poet, writer, and nurse from Brandon, Manitoba. She studied Psychology and English at Brandon University, and Nursing at Assiniboine Community College. Her work has appeared in *NewMyths.com, Love Letters to Poe,* Black Hare Press, and several other literary magazines and anthologies. She is forthcoming with Off Topic.

Twitter: @reneecronley

Rosetta Yorke

Author of *Sweeter Than Success, Love Burns, Dying to Love* and *Love and War*

Rosetta Yorke is a North Yorkshire novelist and short fiction writer who firmly believes in romance and happy endings. She is working on her debut novel, a timeslip romance set mostly in eighteenth-century Venice.

Twitter: @RosettaYorke

S. Jade Path

Author of *Forever, Your Smile*

S. Jade Path is an author of short fiction and a creator of dark poetry. She has had a life-long obsession with crawling into the depths of the psyche and forging shadows into words. Her work parallels this penchant for delving into the fantastical and strolling amongst demons.

Website: linktr.ee/SJadePath

S.T. May

Author of *Ascent of Man, Perfect Recall,* and *Amore Roma*

S.T May grew up near Stonehenge, lived many years by the sea in Sussex, then moved to Coventry and finally Nottingham, both sadly as far from the beach as possible in Britain. They contributed to the record-breaking anthology *81 words* and *A Compendium of Enigmatic Species.*

Selene Moor

Author of *Café Crossroads, Days Long Gone, Fairy Tale Lover, Take Me* and *Hatfields and McCoys*

Shawna Renée Lewis

Author of *Every Ten Years* and *Finally*

Shawna (she/her) lives in Northern California with her three cats, Hans, Lucky, and Shadow, who keep her laughing with their crazy shenanigans. Shawna received her MA in English and Creative Writing from Southern New Hampshire University. When not writing she is working on her artwork or socialising feral cats.

Twitter: @ShawnaReneeArt

Tam Lynn

Author of *Technological Wonder, Break-Out, Closure, Playing Tourist* and *Divortium*

Tess P.

Author of *The Clock Decides*

Tess published *Secret Whispers* in 2021 —a delicious collection of light/dark poetry.
Secret Portrait —a deadly mix of poetry and prose, is out 2023.
In between writing, you'll find her wandering woodland, taking weird photos, snorkelling seas, or exploring cities. Follow her Twitter chat: @Tess_2020 Or contact: tesspoetry@yahoo.com

Twitter: @tess_2020

Tiffiny Rose Allen

Author of *Whisper My Name in Bedsheets*

Tiffiny Rose Allen is a writer and poet. Originally from the state of Florida, she started writing at an early age and self-published her first collection of poetry *Leave the Dreaming to the Flowers* at the age of 18.

Website: dreamsinhiding.wixsite.com/mysite

Velian Dusk

Author of *Come Find Me, Rekindled Warmth, Out of the Zone, Blood Vow* and As the World Spins

Velian Dusk is an independent writer who specialises in dark fantasy and Omegaverse fiction. He's recently co-authored and self-published his second book, *The Regent's Key*, on Amazon. Velian is currently writing, illustrating poetry books, and pursuing his Masters in English. He's a genderqueer trans man and a proud LGBTQIA+ advocate.

Website: vincenthunterofficial.wordpress.com/velian-dusk

About the Publisher

DARK ROSE PRESS is an independent boutique publisher of dark romantic fiction.

We are founded on the premise that dark hearts love differently.

We are an inclusive publisher, committed to developing and amplifying diverse voices and perspectives.

Connect: *linktr.ee/darkrosepress*
Website: *www.darkrosepress.com*

Acknowledgements

When Dark Rose Press first opened our doors in 2021, we never envisioned the flood of support we'd receive from the romance writing community.

We have been truly humbled by the number of submissions we've received for our first set of anthologies—Destined Drabbles (nearly 500!).

To the writers who have come along with us on this journey and have shared with us their bite-sized tales. We thank you from the bottom of our hearts.

A special thank you to the read team for volunteering your time and talents to our endeavours. Your input is priceless.

To our families and friends, collaborators, myriad baristas, and everyone else who has helped behind the scenes: we couldn't have done it without you.

Special thanks to our Patreon supporters, your support will help fund future publications and paid calls. Check out our Patreon here—patreon.com/darkrosepress.

And to you, dear reader, we hope you enjoyed these tales, and if you did, don't forget to leave a review.

Cheers,

The Dark Rose Press Team

Printed in Great Britain
by Amazon

23427973R00081